D1246086

BEWARE THE KING!

ReadZone Books Limited

First published in this edition 2015

© copyright in the text Stewart Ross, 1996
© copyright in this edition ReadZone Books 2015

First published 1996 by Evans Brothers Ltd

The right of the Author to be identified as the Author of this work has been asserted by the Author in accordance with the Copyright, Designs and Patents Act 1988.

Printed in Malta by Melita Press

Every attempt has been made by the Publisher to secure appropriate permissions for material reproduced in this book. If there has been any oversight we will be happy to rectify the situation in future editions or reprints. Written submissions should be made to the Publishers.

British Library Cataloguing in Publication Data (CIP) is available for this title.

All rights reserved. No part of this publication may be reproduced, stored in a retrieval system, or transmitted, in any form, or by any means, electronic, mechanical, photocopying, or otherwise, without the prior permission of ReadZone Books Limited.

ISBN 978 1 78322 559 0

Visit our website: www.readzonebooks.com

BEWARE THE KING!

Stewart Ross

CONTENTS

TO THE READER

Beware the King! is a story. It is based on history.
The main events in the book really happened. But some
of the details, such as what people said, are made up.
I hope this makes the story easier to read. I also hope
that *Beware the King!* will get you interested in real
history. When you have finished, perhaps you will want
to find out more about Henry the Eighth and his wives!

Stewart Ross

THE STORY SO FAR ...

THE WAR OF THE ROSES

Between 1455 and 1487, the Wars of Roses raged in England. The family of Lancaster (the red rose) battled for the throne with the family of York (the white rose). A Lancastrian king was followed by two Yorkists.

In 1485 Henry Tudor fought for the Lancastrians. He defeated the Yorkist king, Richard III. Richard was killed and Henry Tudor became King Henry VII. He married a Yorkist princess and the Wars of the Roses came to an end.

THE TUDORS

Henry VII rules carefully and wisely. He saved money, avoided war and made good marriages for his children. His daughter married the king of Scotland. His elder son Arthur married the Spanish princess Katherine of Aragon.

Prince Arthur died young. His brother Henry got permission from the Pope and married Arthur's widow, Katherine. Henry VII died in 1509 and Henry VIII became king. He was young, talented and popular. He was a strong supporter of the Church.

HENRY AND KATHERINE

To begin with, Henry and Katherine got on well. They had just one daughter, Mary. Henry grew bored with his wife. He was also desperate for a son. He feared that, unless he had a son, the terrible civil wars would return after his death.

RELIGIOUS RUMBLINGS

At the time of Henry VIII, the Church was not popular. The priests seemed rich and lazy. The head of the Church, the Pope, appeared more like a king than a priest. In the end, some people were so fed up that they set up churches of their own. The Pope had no control over them.

TIME LINE
CE (Common Era)

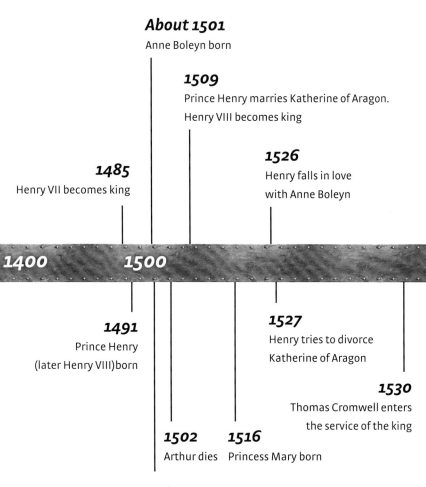

About 1501
Anne Boleyn born

1509
Prince Henry marries Katherine of Aragon.
Henry VIII becomes king

1526
Henry falls in love
with Anne Boleyn

1485
Henry VII becomes king

1400

1500

1491
Prince Henry
(later Henry VIII) born

1527
Henry tries to divorce
Katherine of Aragon

1530
Thomas Cromwell enters
the service of the king

1502
Arthur dies

1516
Princess Mary born

1501
Katherine of Aragon
marries Prince Arthur

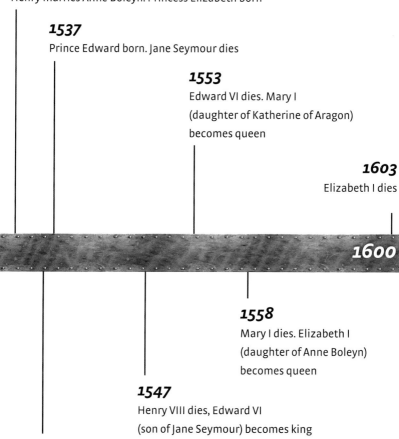

1533
Henry divorced from Katherine of Aragon.
Henry marries Anne Boleyn. Princess Elizabeth born

1537
Prince Edward born. Jane Seymour dies

1553
Edward VI dies. Mary I
(daughter of Katherine of Aragon)
becomes queen

1603
Elizabeth I dies

1600

1558
Mary I dies. Elizabeth I
(daughter of Anne Boleyn)
becomes queen

1547
Henry VIII dies, Edward VI
(son of Jane Seymour) becomes king

1536
Katherine of Aragon dies. Anne Boleyn
executed. Henry VIII marries Jane Seymour

11

PORTRAIT GALLERY

Henry VIII, the second king of England from the Tudor family

Katherine, the Spanish princess who married Prince Arthur and then King Henry

Anne Boleyn, a lively young lady of Henry VIII's court

Mary Boleyn, Anne's elder sister

Jane Seymour, a lady-in-waiting

Chapter 1

THE SECRET

Anne Boleyn was bubbling with excitement. Tournaments were her favourite sport. She liked the costumes, the trumpets and the crowds. Above all, she liked the thrills. She loved to see the brave and handsome knights charging each other on horseback.

The finest knights in Europe were here today. It was going to be the best tournament of all.

Anne sat down beside her sister Mary and looked around. The ladies of the court filled the stand. Some were chatting, some were waving. They were a magnificent sight in their long, bright dresses. Queen Katherine was at the front. Her ten-year-old daughter sat beside her.

Anne looked carefully at the queen. She was an elegant woman, but she was not very beautiful. She was plump and serious. Her red-gold hair was tied up in a bun on the back of her head. Anne thought she looked rather boring.

I'm much prettier than her, Anne thought. And much more fun. She smiled to herself.

Mary noticed her sister's look. 'What are you smiling at, Anne?' she asked.

'Nothing', Anne replied. 'Nothing that matters, anyway.'

'Come off it!' Mary laughed. She knew her younger sister well. 'Tell me what you were thinking.'

Anne leaned towards her. 'I was looking at the queen', she whispered. 'She's such a frump!'

Mary was shocked. 'Shhh! Don't say things like that, Anne! You'll be in serious trouble if anyone hears you.'

'I don't care!' Anne replied. 'Anyway, it's true. Everyone knows it. Even the king finds her boring!'

At that moment the trumpets sounded. The tournament had begun.

The first fight was between an English champion and a handsome young knight from France. Most of the ladies thought the Frenchman was very dashing. Some waved their handkerchiefs at him. He bowed and waved back.

Soon the two knights were ready. The trumpets blared. The men lowered their lances and charged.

Horses' hooves thundered on the ground. Everyone held their breath. The knights met with a great crash. The Frenchman's lance broke in two. But the Englishman's lance slammed into his opponent's shield.

The Frenchman was thrown right out of the saddle. He landed on the ground with a clatter and lay still. A lady on Anne's right let out a scream of horror.

'Poor man!' cried Mary. 'I do hope he's all right. He was my champion.'

Most of the ladies had a champion. He was their favourite knight and they wanted him to win. Some of the knights had the names of their wives or lady friends woven on to their coats.

Tournaments were very romantic.

In a few minutes, the French knight got to his feet. He had a broken arm, but he was not too badly hurt.

'Thank goodness!' Mary said when she saw her hero walking away. 'I thought for a minute he had been killed.'

Anne did not seem very interested.

'Wasn't he your champion too, Anne?' asked Mary. 'After all, you did live in France once. I thought you liked French knights.'

'No, he was not my champion', Anne said proudly. 'I liked French knights once. But not anymore.'

She turned to see who was fighting next.

Mary was a married woman. She chose a champion just for fun. But the twenty-four-year-old Anne Boleyn was not married. She was one of the prettiest and liveliest of the queen's ladies-in-waiting. Her family expected her to find a husband soon. Many young men took a fancy to her.

Mary was dying to know who Anne's favourite was. 'Come on', she teased. 'Tell me the name of your hero.'

'No', Anne smiled. 'It's a secret.'

But it was not a secret for much longer.

Chapter 2

'I DARE NOT TELL'

It was King Henry's turn. This was the moment everyone had been waiting for. All eyes turned towards the good-looking king as he rode into the tournament ground. The crowd clapped and cheered.

'Long live King Hal!' people called as he rode up and down before the stands. He bowed gracefully to the crowd. He was tall and strong – the perfect figure of a king.

But what the crowd most wanted to see was the name of the lady on his coat. Was it Queen Katherine?

Mary leaned forward. Her eyes were rather weak. 'What does it say?' she asked her sister. 'Is he fighting for the queen?'

Anne did not reply. Instead, the lady on Mary's other side read out the words: 'I dare not tell'.

Mary looked puzzled. 'What does that mean?' she asked.

The lady explained. 'It means, my dear, that the king does not want to say who he is fighting for. Certainly, it is not the queen.' She lowered her voice. 'They say he has a new lady friend!'

Mary was not surprised. King Henry was fond of Queen Katherine, but he did not love her. He was always chasing other women. Mary herself had been his friend for a time. She wondered who his new lady was.

By now the king was right in front of them. He pulled gently on his horse's reins and stopped. Mary could not believe her eyes.

Henry's face broke into a broad smile. He lifted his hand and waved. Mary waved back. Then she realised – he was not waving at her.

He was looking straight at Anne.

A few seconds later, Henry rode on. Mary turned to her sister. Anne was blushing. All of a sudden, Mary realised what was going on.

'Oh Anne!' she muttered, taking her sister's hand. 'Why didn't you tell me?'

'Tell you what?' Anne replied.

'That the king is your champion.'

Anne laughed but said nothing.

'Does he love you?' Mary asked quickly. 'Does he want you to be his lady friend? Do you want to be his friend? Come on, you must tell me what's going on!'

Anne looked into her sister's face. She had stopped smiling. 'Yes, Henry does love me', she said quietly. 'And, yes, he does want me to be his lady friend. But no, I will not accept.'

'What?' Mary cried. 'Why ever not? It is such an honour, and he is so handsome and –'

'Listen!' Anne interrupted. 'I do not want to be his friend.' Her voice was calm. 'I want to be his wife.'

Mary could not believe her ears. 'What did you say?'

'I said I want to be queen.'

'But Henry has a queen!' Mary spluttered.

Anne looked proud and determined. 'So what? I will be his new queen. Queen Anne.'

Tears came into Mary's eyes. 'Oh Anne!' she said. 'What are you saying? Be careful, sister! Beware the king! Oh, beware the king!'

Chapter 3

A PUNISHMENT FROM GOD

Henry was crazy about Anne Boleyn. He sent her presents of jewellery and clothes. He sat next to her at meals and danced with her long into the night. He took her hunting. Never for one minute did he like to be out of her sight. If other men paid attention to her, he grew angry and jealous.

Soon the whole country was talking about the king's new favourite. People gossiped about Anne in shops and pubs and at court. Much of what they said was not very polite. They called her a shameless woman who was taking the king away from Queen Katherine.

The queen was patient and kind. The people loved her.

Henry and Katherine had been married for years. They had one daughter. The queen was now too old to have any more children. This did not please Henry at all.

One day, riding back from a hunting trip, the king drew level with Anne. She looked up and smiled at him.

'Have you enjoyed the hunting, my lord?' she asked.

'Yes and no', he answered. He leaned across and kissed her on the cheek.

'What a strange answer!' she laughed. 'What does it mean, my lord?'

Henry sighed. 'You know what it means, my lovely Anne! I killed five deer. That was good hunting. But I did not catch the "dear" I really want.'

Anne glanced across at him. She pretended not to understand.

'Which deer have you not caught?' she asked.

'You, my only dear!' Henry said.

'But you have caught me', Anne laughed. 'I am your best friend. I love you.'

The king became serious. 'Anne, I want a son. I need a son to be king when I die. England will need a king.'

She thought for a moment. 'Only your wife can give you a son, Henry. You know that.'

'But my wife is too old!' he cried. 'She cannot give me a son!'

Startled by the sudden noise, his horse jumped forward. He pulled on the reins and waited for Anne to catch up.

'My lord', she said softly, 'If Queen Katherine cannot give you a son, what are you going to do about it?'

'I don't know', Henry muttered. 'I just don't know.'

He seemed very troubled.

Henry's bad mood lasted for weeks. He was grumpy with his advisors. He shouted at his courtiers. Once or twice he was even rude to his queen. He told her she had let him down. He should never have married her, he said crossly. Katherine made no reply. Henry had been angry with her before, but he always got over it.

In the end, Henry made up his mind. One evening after supper he went to find Anne. She was sitting sewing with a group of ladies-in-waiting. The king sent them out of the room.

When they had gone, he took Anne in his arms. 'My love', he said, 'I have come to ask you a question. An important question.'

She felt her heart beating faster. Was this the moment she had been waiting for?

'Well, my lord', she replied. 'What do you want to know?'

He held her tightly. 'You will say yes, won't you?' he asked.

She looked into his eyes. 'It depends what you want, Henry. But you know I always do my best to please you.'

He took a deep breath. 'Will you be my wife, Anne?'

'Your wife? Yes, my love!' she cried, almost without thinking. 'Of course I will be your wife. Your queen, too.'

'Wonderful!' roared the king. 'We shall be married and spend the rest of our lives together – and have dozens of sons!'

After he had kissed her, Anne moved away. The smile fell from her face. 'But you are already married, Henry', she said. 'What about Queen Katherine?'

'Bother the boring old woman!' he growled. 'I shall divorce her! I should not have married her in the first place. That is why I have no sons. It is a punishment from God for marrying her.'

Anne's dreams were coming true at last. She wanted to rush off and tell her sister the news. But she had to be careful.

'Is our engagement a secret?' she asked.

Henry thought for a moment. 'Yes, for the moment. We must keep it secret until Katherine is out of the way.'

'What a lovely secret!' Anne sighed. She came forward and put her arms round Henry's neck.

'My dearest Henry', she whispered, 'it is the best secret in the world!'

Chapter 4

MR CROMWELL'S PLAN

Henry met his wife in the garden of Hampton Court Palace. She was walking alone, enjoying the fresh morning air. When she saw him, she stopped and smiled.

Henry marched up to her. He looked very large and very determined.

'Good morning Katherine', he said as if he was talking to someone he hardly knew. 'I have something to say.'

The queen nodded. 'I know', she said.

Her answer annoyed him. 'Good', he went on. 'Then I won't use many words.' He looked around the garden to see that no one was listening. 'We must get divorced.'

Katherine sat down on a bench. 'Really?' she asked. 'Because you have fallen in love? I am not stupid, Henry. I have seen you and Anne Boleyn.'

'The king shuffled his feet on the gravel path. 'Right', he said quickly. 'So you agree? We'll be divorced as soon as possible.'

'Agree?' cried Katherine. 'My dear Henry, of course I don't agree! I am your wife. I love you. Mistress Boleyn is younger than me. She is lively and quite pretty, too.' She looked her husband straight in the face. 'But she will not make a good queen, Henry. The people do not like her, and she will soon be old, like me.'

Henry was shaking with rage. 'How dare you!' he shouted.

Before he could say anything else, Katherine interrupted him.

'Listen, Henry! We were married in a church, before God. Marriage is for life. Besides, the Pope is in charge of the Church. Only he can give us a divorce, and I know he will not do so.'

Henry stared at her. His eyes were small and hard, like stones.

'Stay with me, Henry', Katherine asked softly. 'Please. Your new love will soon pass.'

The king exploded with anger. 'No, it will not!' he yelled. 'Stay with you? I would rather stay with an old cat! I will get a divorce, Pope or no Pope! Just you see!'

He stormed off to play tennis.

Katherine was right. The Pope did not give Henry a divorce. The king begged and threatened, but it made no difference. The Pope was head of the Church. Divorce was impossible without his help.

Several years passed. The love between Anne and Henry remained as strong as ever. But they could not marry, and Henry did not have a son. He grew desperate.

At this point, the king found a new advisor. His name was Thomas Cromwell. Cromwell was clever and crafty. He would stop at nothing to give his master what he wanted.

'If you want a divorce, my lord', he told the king,

'then leave it to me. Cromwell can fix everything, my lord. Everything.'

Cromwell did fix it. His plan was simple. The king would take over from the Pope. Henry would be head of the Church of England.

Henry thought it was a great idea. He got Cromwell to write new laws to put the king in charge of the Church of England.

Anyone who disagreed was killed.

Chapter 5

HA! HA!

Henry had got his way at last. The Church of England said the king had never been married to Katherine. He was now free to find a new wife. He gave Anne her own palace. She was no longer called Anne Boleyn but the Marquess of Pembroke.

Katherine was moved out of her palace into a small house in the country. Soon she became ill.

The people of England felt more sorry for Katherine than ever. Few of them had anything good to say about the Marquess of Pembroke.

Henry and Anne married in secret. The wedding took place one winter morning, while it was still dark. It was not the sort of service Anne had been expecting. She wanted a cathedral and cheering crowds and trumpets. But Henry was afraid of his people.

When the service was over, Henry took Anne in his arms.

'After all these years!' he said, smiling like a little boy. 'Now you are my own wife! We will have a son!'

'My own Henry!' Anne sighed. She could hardly believe she was married at last. 'Yes, we will have a son. And I will be crowned queen, won't I, my love?'

Henry laughed. 'Of course! As soon as possible! It will be the finest coronation the country has ever seen!

Specially for my beloved Anne!'

Anne was crowned four months later.

As Henry promised, the coronation was splendid. All the important people in the land were there, wearing their finest clothes. Anne looked wonderful in a crimson gown and a crown of pearls. The drinking fountains flowed with free wine. Golden arches were built over the streets. Banners with the initials 'H' and 'A' hung from the poles. Choirs sang, poets wrote special verses, girls danced, music played. Huge crowds turned out to watch.

But they did not cheer.

Anne counted only ten people who called out, 'God save the queen!' Worse still, when the people saw 'H' and 'A' on the banners, they shouted out 'HA! HA!' as if they were laughing.

The new queen was disappointed. She became more proud than ever.

After the coronation there was a huge banquet. Fifty-one courses were served. Anne ate only three. She did not want to put on weight.

When they were alone, the king asked kindly, 'Was that the best day of your life, my love?'

'Maybe,' she replied. 'But it's a pity the people do not like me.'

'They will', he said cheerfully, 'in time.'

Anne smiled. 'Yes, you are right, Henry. They will like me better when they hear my news.'

'Your news?' Henry held his breath.

'I am going to have a baby', she said quietly.

The king was delighted. He jumped into the air and shouted, 'A baby? No! A son! Hooray! I am going to have a son! At last, I am going to have a son!'

He took hold of Anne and danced with her round the room.

Chapter 6

PRINCESS ELIZABETH

Henry and Anne were very happy after their marriage. The king was excited about the baby who was to be born. He made sure the queen was always comfortable. The best doctors in the land looked after her. People who knew Henry well said he had never been in a better mood. Soon, he boasted, his wish would come true. He was going to have a son.

Henry never saw his first wife, Katherine. She was shut away in the country. She spent much time praying. In the eyes of God, she said, she was still Henry's wife. Many people agreed with her. Anne had nothing to do with her.

In September the time came for Anne to have her baby. It was born at about three o'clock in the afternoon.

Anne was tired but full of joy.

'Let me look at my son', she asked.

The nurse frowned.

Anne pushed the hair back from her brow. 'What's the matter?' she demanded. 'Is the baby sick?'

The nurse took a deep breath. 'Nothing is the matter, Your Majesty', she answered. 'Your baby is healthy. But it is not a boy. You have given birth to a princess.'

Anne lay back on the pillows. A princess! she thought.

Oh dear! Whatever will Henry say? Her eyes filled with tears.

That evening the king came to see his wife and baby daughter. He smiled when he came into the room. But Anne knew he was disappointed.

'Congratulations, my dearest!' he said. He bent over and gave her a kiss. 'What a beautiful baby!'

'Yes', she said weakly. 'But I'm afraid it is not the boy you wanted.'

A dark look passed over Henry's face. 'No matter', he said cheerfully. 'We are both young. We will have plenty more children. The next one will be a prince, I'm sure!'

From that day onwards, Henry's love for Anne began to cool.

The princess was christened Elizabeth. She was a bonny baby, with beautiful red hair. Anne loved her dearly and did everything she could to make her happy. She did not see so much of Henry now. Most of the time he seemed to be busy with other matters.

Sometimes Anne wondered where he got to.

In time, the queen became pregnant again. But the child died before it was born. The next year, the same thing happened.

There was not much happiness in Anne's life. The people still did not like her. Sometimes she quarrelled with Henry. Even the courtiers took less notice of her. She spent a lot of time with Elizabeth. She liked playing with her dogs and ordering new clothes. She became more serious, too. Courtiers noticed she often carried a prayer book. She gave money to poor widows and students.

One afternoon Anne was wandering through the palace. Most of the courtiers looked rather gloomy. Queen Katherine had died a few days earlier. She had been buried that morning.

Poor woman, Anne thought. She was sorry that she had made the old queen so miserable. She remembered the words of her sister all those years ago: 'Beware the king!'

It had not been a foolish warning, Anne thought. At least, not for Katherine.

Anne was pregnant again. This time, she hoped, she would have a son. She decided to go and have a chat with Henry. She entered his rooms without knocking.

The king was in a large chair. Sitting on his knee, with her arms round his neck, was a lady. It was Jane Seymour, one of the queen's ladies-in-waiting.

Anne went wild with rage.

'Henry!' she screamed. 'What are you doing? How dare you! What an insult!'

Henry stood up and sent Jane out of the room. He looked very sheepish.

'Peace, sweetheart!' he mumbled. 'Don't get so excited about nothing.'

'Nothing!' yelled Anne. 'You call that nothing?'

Henry tried to take her hand. She turned away.

'Hush!' he said. 'Don't get so angry. Remember our baby. You will make yourself ill.'

'I don't care!' Anne shouted. She was almost crying. 'How could you behave like that with one of my own ladies-in-waiting?'

'Sorry', Henry muttered.

Anne did not reply. With tears streaming down her face, she ran out the room.

That evening her baby was born. It was born too early and did not live.

The nurse said it was a boy.

Chapter 7

THE TOWER

Cromwell was sitting at a table with a pen in his hand. He was taking notes on a piece of paper. The king walked up and down beside him. He was fatter now and not so handsome.

'You see my problem, Cromwell?' he asked.

'Yes, Your Majesty. It is very clear', Cromwell answered. He jotted something down.

'Well, what are you going to do about it?' the king demanded.

Cromwell put down his pen. 'I can fix everything, Your Majesty. Just leave it to me.'

Henry stood behind him. 'Are you sure?'

'No problem, Your Majesty. Did I sort out your divorce?'

'You did', Henry said. 'You got Katherine out of the way. But what will you do about Anne? I should never have married her. God is punishing me by not giving me a son. I must have a son, you know.'

Cromwell smiled. 'Of course, Your Majesty. The whole of England wants you to have a son. But first we must get rid of Queen Anne.'

Henry started walking up and down again. 'How?' he asked. 'How can you get rid of her?'

'I think we need to cut off her head, Your Majesty.'

'What!' Henry was shocked. 'What for?'

'She is a traitor, Your Majesty. She is plotting to kill you.'

Henry walked back to the table. He did not believe Cromwell. But the truth did not matter to him.

'Really?' he asked. 'Can you prove it?'

'I will prove it, Your Majesty. In a law court.'

A grin spread across the king's face. 'Good! Very good! Go ahead then, Mister Cromwell. Let's finish off Anne as quickly as possible. Then I will be free to marry again. And have a son!'

Anne knew that things were going badly wrong. Henry avoided her. When they met, he was rough and unkind. Once, she heard a courtier talking about her. He called her a 'thin old woman'. She went straight to the mirror. The man was right, she realized. She was not beautiful any longer.

Henry spent more and more time with Jane Seymour. At first Anne complained. Sometimes she lost her temper. It made no difference. She now understood how Queen Katherine had felt.

Anne wondered whether Henry wanted to divorce her. But he had other plans. He did not want to divorce his second queen. He wanted her right out of the way, for ever.

The blow fell one May morning. Anne was watching a tennis match. A messenger told her that some of the king's advisors wanted to talk with her. When she went to see them, they said they had heard wicked stories about her. She was not to leave her rooms.

During lunch that afternoon, Anne's uncle came into the room. He was carrying a large piece of paper. His face was grim.

Anne turned white. 'Uncle', she asked, 'What's the paper in your hand?'

'It is a command from the king', he replied. 'You are under arrest. I must take you to the Tower of London.'

Anne stood up slowly. 'Very well', she said quietly. 'If that is what His Majesty wants, I will obey.'

Guards took the queen to the Tower in a boat down the River Thames. When she arrived, she fell on her knees.

'Jesus have mercy on me!' she wept. 'I am innocent! O my poor mother! O my poor daughter! Mercy, I pray you! Mercy!'

Half laughing, half crying, she was led into the Tower.

Back in the palace, King Henry was planning his wedding to Jane Seymour.

Anne was kept in a few rooms with some of her close friends. They comforted her and gradually she settled down. Later, she learned that Cromwell said she was a traitor. She and her men friends had plotted to kill the king, he lied. Her own brother had helped her.

Anne knew it was not true. The men said it was all lies, too. But no one believed them. Anne now understood that when Henry really wanted something, he always got it. Now he wanted Jane Seymour.

Chapter 8

'HAVE PITY ON MY SOUL!'

Anne was taken to a law court in the Tower. A large crowd came to watch. Many more gathered outside. The king was nowhere to be seen.

There was nothing Anne could do to save herself. When everyone had spoken, her uncle stood up. His face was pale and grim.

'We all agree that you plotted to kill His Majesty the King', he announced. 'You are a traitor. Your punishment is either to be burned alive, or to have your head cut off. The king will decide which.'

Anne lifted up her eyes and said calmly, 'O God Our Father. You know the truth. I am innocent, but I am ready to die.'

She spoke for several minutes. She said she had never meant to hurt the king. She was sorry, too, for the poor men who also had to die.

'But because the king wants it', she ended, 'I will die with them. We will all meet in heaven.'

It was a fine speech. Many people wept. Even Anne's enemies pitied her.

For the first time in her life, Anne Boleyn was popular.

Henry had some pity in him. He did not want Anne to be burned. Instead, he ordered her to be killed by having her head cut off. He wanted the best executioner in Europe to do the deed. He was a Frenchman who had to make a special trip from France.

The execution was planned for nine o'clock in the morning on 18th May. From her window Anne watched the workmen building a large platform on the lawn. In the middle they placed a wooden chopping block.

As Anne looked at it, she thought of the tournament all those years ago. Henry had looked so handsome then. So dashing and kind and loving. What a fool she had been! Mary's words of warning rang in her ears: 'Be careful, sister! Beware the king! Oh, beware the king!'

If only I had listened! Anne said to herself. If only I had listened!

Anne did not sleep that night. She stayed awake and said her prayers.

Just before nine in the morning, a messenger told her that the executioner had not arrived. The execution would now take place at midday. Anne was quite calm. She was ready to die, so it did not matter when.

Later, Anne was told the executioner still had not come. She would now die the next morning. The news upset her. She spent another night without sleep.

After breakfast on 19th May, the jailer came into Anne's rooms. 'Madam', he said, 'The hour has come. Get yourself ready.'

Anne thanked him. She gave him her purse. It had twenty pounds in it. Some of the money was to pay the executioner. The rest was for the poor.

Three thousand people came to see the execution. They groaned loudly when Anne appeared. Some of them started weeping. Anne looked behind her as she walked on to the platform. She hoped Henry would change his mind and come to her rescue.

He did not appear.

On the platform Anne made a short speech. Once again, she swore she was innocent. She was sorry if she had upset anyone. Finally, she asked the people to pray for her.

A guard gave her a black handkerchief. She tied it round her eyes. Then she knelt down and put her neck on the block.

The executioner picked up his sword.

'O Lord God, have pity on my soul', Anne prayed.

The executioner ended her life with one swift blow. He picked up her head and cried out, 'So die all the king's enemies!'

The guns of the Tower fired to let people know what had happened.

When Henry heard the sound, he galloped off to find Jane Seymour. She was his latest love. She was going to give him a son.

He never mentioned Anne's name again.

THE HISTORY FILE

WHAT HAPPENED NEXT?

Henry's marriages

Henry married Jane Seymour eleven days after Anne's death. They had a son, Edward. Jane died shortly afterwards. Henry then married a fourth wife, a European princess named Anne of Cleves. He found her so unattractive that he divorced her almost immediately and married Catherine Howard.

Catherine had no children and met with the same fate as Anne Boleyn. She was beheaded in 1542. Finally, Henry married a sixth wife, Catherine Parr. They were still married when he died in 1547. The marriage was childless.

Henry's children

When his father died, Prince Edward, the son of Jane Seymour, ruled as Edward VI. He was a sickly boy and died at the age of sixteen. Mary, the daughter of Katherine of Aragon, then became queen. She married the king of Spain but had no children. She brought back the Roman Catholic Church and executed many Protestants. She was not popular. When Mary died in 1558, Anne Boleyn's daughter Elizabeth came to the throne.

The reign of Elizabeth I was long and successful. The country prospered and won victories against Spain.

The most famous was the defeat of the Spanish Armada. Elizabeth never married, however, and when she died in 1603, the rule of the Tudors came to an end.

The Church of England

The Church of England, which Henry VIII set up, survives to this day. When Henry took over the Church, he seized much of its wealth. In particular, he got rid of the many monasteries that had dotted the land since medieval times. The ruins of many of these monasteries can still be seen. Some are very beautiful.

The Church of England became a Protestant church in the reign of Edward VI. Mary made it Catholic again. Elizabeth brought it back to Protestantism, and it has remained Protestant ever since.

HOW DO WE KNOW?

There is a huge amount of information about the story of Henry VIII and Anne Boleyn. We can still read the letters that he wrote to her, but unfortunately her letters to him were destroyed. There are many other letters and reports written during Anne's lifetime. Some of the most interesting were written by foreigners living in England. They wrote home telling people what was going on.

We can also visit some of the places where Anne went, including Hever Castle in Kent and the gloomy Tower of London! We have paintings of Anne, too. It is interesting to compare those that were done when she was young with those painted towards the end of her life.

There are plenty of modern books about Anne, too. More has been written about her than any other of Henry's wives. She has also been the subject of a film, *Anne of 1000 Days*. It is fun, but not very accurate!

NEW WORDS

Advisor
Someone who gives advice; a helper.

Arrest
Take to prison.

Banquet
A huge feast.

Christen
Give a name to a baby in a church.

Coronation
When someone is crowned.

Court
The king's household.

Courtier
Someone who spends time at court.

Crowned
Made king or queen by putting a crown on their head.

Divorce
The end of a marriage.

Engagement
An agreement to get married.

Executioner
Someone who kills people when the law says they must die.

Knight
A soldier who fights on horseback.

Lady-in-waiting
A woman who looks after a queen.

Lance
A spear.

Marquess
A female noble.

Pope
The head of the Roman Catholic Church.

Pregnant
Expecting a baby.

Protestants
Christians who *protested* against the Roman Catholic Church and broke away to set up churches of their own.

Roman Catholics

Members of the traditional Christian Church that was headed by the Pope.

The Tower of London

A great fortress on the east side of the city.

Tournament

A fight done for sport with people watching.

Traitor

Someone who betrays or tries to harm the king or queen.

Tudor

The family name of Henry VIII.